The Story of
Ishmael
Munch

By **Diane Ashley-Barlow**
**Illustrated by David Jernigan
and Nancy Bailey**

Proctor Publications, LLC • Ann Arbor • Michigan • USA

Proctor Publications, LLC
P.O. Box 2498
Ann Arbor, Michigan 48106, USA
(800) 343-3034

Library of Congress Catalog Number: 2002102040

Publisher's Cataloging-in-Publication
(Provided by Quality Books, Inc.)

Barlow, Diane Ashley.
    The Story of Ishmael Munch / by Diane Ashley Barlow — 1st ed.
    p.cm.
    SUMMARY: Ishmael, a newborn lamb, tries to discover
who he is.
    LCCN 2002102040
    ISBN 1-928623-14-X

    1. Self-acceptance—Juvenile fiction.
2. Self-perception—Juvenile fiction. 3. Individuality—
Juvenile fiction. 4 Lambs—Juvenile fiction.
[1. Self-acceptance—Fiction. 2. Self-perception—Fiction.
3. Individuality—Fiction. 4. Sheep—Fiction.
5. Animals—Infancy—Fiction.]   I. Title.

PZ7.B25075Sto 2002   [E]
                  QB133-387

Printed in Canada

Dedicated to

Ann LaRee

who loved animals, too

and

to my brother Bob

who has always believed in me.

One little lamb was much smaller than any of the other lambs born that bitter cold night in a dark corner of the barn. When Mrs. Farmer came to the barn in the morning she found him shivering and cold, too weak to be warmed even by his woolly mother, too tiny to reach, even on tiptoe, the milk he needed.

"You poor little fellow," said Mrs. Farmer. "You're so tiny. So cold. I'll take you into the house with me." She gathered up the little lamb and tucked him into the front of her heavy coat for the trip across the yard to the farmhouse.

"First of all we must warm you up," said Mrs. Farmer. She bustled here, she bustled there, around the cozy kitchen. She found a basket just the right size and into it she placed a knitted shawl. Then, Mrs. Farmer tucked the lamb down into the woolly softness and set the  basket on the rug by the stove while she heated some milk for him. When the bottle of milk was ready she scooped up the lamb, still wrapped in the shawl, and sat in the rocking chair

by the stove to feed him. "My, aren't you a tiny one and so hungry. Well, let's see what we can do about that."

She chattered to him as she rocked on the rug by the stove. Soon the little lamb, warmed by the milk and her arms cuddling him in the shawl, fell asleep. Later, when he awoke he was back in the basket by the stove. Mrs. Farmer was not in the chair beside him. He was alone and suddenly afraid.

"Maa Maa," he cried out, his eyes frantically searching the huge room for Mrs. Farmer. "Maa Maa," he called again, though it would have sounded very much like 'Mama' to anyone who chanced to be listening. Mrs. Farmer was listening. She crossed the room to the basket and smiled down into his brown eyes.

"Big round eyes, purple tongue, no teeth whatever . . .

'Mama' indeed," she said and laughed. "Well, I believe I'll call you Ishmael," she said and laughed once more. Ishmael felt warm and safe again.

Ishmael was happy in his basket by the stove. The shawl was cozy, the kitchen was warm, the milk was absolutely delicious, and Maa Maa was close by.

Ishmael's tiny brown body grew rounder. Stronger. His spindly black sticklegs grew longer and he tottered happily about as he followed Mrs. Farmer around the kitchen.

As Ishmael grew bigger he began to think bigger thoughts. He began to wonder just who he was. He didn't look like Mrs. Farmer, though he knew she was his Maa Maa. He didn't look like the bark-ing dogs who ran so busily here and there about the farm. He 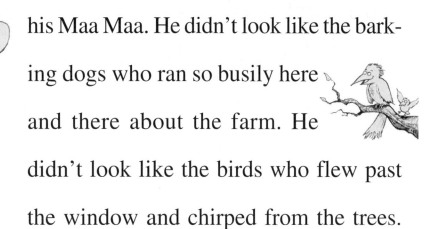 didn't look like the birds who flew past the window and chirped from the trees. And he certainly didn't look like the wise old cat who sat on the window seat to watch the world. But he must be somebody. He simply did not know who.

So Ishmael thought more and more about who he was. His thoughts got bigger and bigger until one day his thoughts were in one big muddle! That was the day Ishmael decided to

ask his question of the wisest one around. That, of course, was Miat, the wise old cat on the windowseat.

Ishmael trotted up to him and asked very politely, "Mr. Miat, could you please tell me who I am? I've been wondering and I simply do not know."

Old Miat regarded Ishmael long and solemnly with his clear green eyes before he answered. "Yes, that is an important thing to know. You must try on many different coats until you find the one that fits." Then he stretched a long, lazy cat-stretch, curled into a ball, and went to sleep.

This didn't help Ishmael's muddle at all. He was still

confused. But he thought and he thought about what old Miat had said and about what coat might fit him. "Well, I guess I'd better get busy trying on coats. Perhaps when one fits I will know who I am."

Ishmael wandered around and around the kitchen looking for a coat to try on. Soon he spied Mrs. Farmer's winter coat hanging on a peg by the door. "I shall try on Maa Maa's coat," he said. "Perhaps I am a farmer, too." But first he had to get the coat down from the peg, and you will remember, I'm sure, that Ishmael was still very little.

Ishmael stood on his back feet and stretched his front

legs as far as he possibly could. He stretched and he stretched but he couldn't even reach the coat with his wee pointed toes. So he backed up a bit, took a running start, and jumped as high as he could, which was pretty high for a little fellow. When he picked himself up from where he had bounced and shook himself off, he saw the coat still hanging on the peg exactly the same as it had been except for the two pointed footprints on it.

"I must get the coat down if I am to try it on," Ishmael muttered. He gazed about the kitchen and saw the chairs neatly placed around the table. "A chair of course. I can reach the coat from a chair, I'm sure." He ran over to the chairs and began to push one to where Maa Maa's coat still hung. But when he stood on the chair he still could not reach the coat.

"Perhaps I need two chairs," he thought. He ran to get another. Ishmael tugged with his mouth. He pushed with his head. He got under the chair and lifted with his brown shoulders. It was very hard work, but finally Ishmael lifted the chair into place. He jumped up onto the chair. As he reached for the coat, the chairs began to tip and to tumble. Everything . . . Ishmael, the chairs, and even the coat came down into a heap.

"Oh dear, trying on coats is very difficult," he said. Ishmael got up, shook himself off and began to put on the coat. The sleeves were longer than his little black legs,

and the coat was much longer than his fuzzy brown body.
Ishmael struggled to put his legs farther into the sleeves. He
wiggled and he squirmed. He pushed and he pulled; the coat
was all around him. He jumped, but not very high this time.
All that hard work made him hungry, so he stopped to nibble
a bit. Ishmael nibbled and nibbled on the fur collar of Mrs.
Farmer's coat. It didn't
taste particularly good,
but as lambs do, he kept right
on nibbling. . . and nibbling. . .
and nibbling. He was still
nibbling as Mrs. Farmer
walked into the kitchen.
There she saw him,

wrapped up in her coat, with the chairs tumbled all about,

nibbling busily on the fur collar

of her coat.

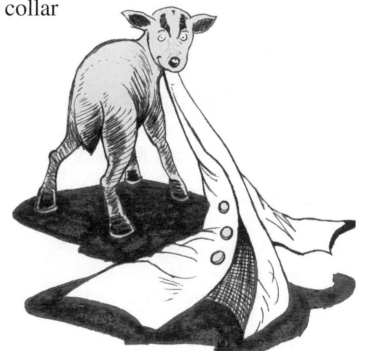

"What are you do-

ing, Ishmael?" cried Mrs.

Farmer.

Ishmael looked up

happily. "Maa Maa,

look," he wanted to tell

her. "I've found a coat to wear! I must be a farmer just like

you."

Mrs. Farmer didn't know how hard he had been work-

ing. She saw the coat in a pile with Ishmael chewing away on

the collar. She saw the chairs knocked over, and she said with a sigh, "Oh Ishmael Munch, you naughty little fellow, you are all mouth! Now, shoo, shoo. I have to pick up this mess."

Ishmael skittered away, then wandered over to the windowseat. His thoughts were all in a muddle again.

"Mr. Miat, I'm sorry to bother you, but I've been trying on coats, and I still don't know who I am. Maa Maa called me  Ishmael Munch. She says that I am all mouth. Please, Sir, what does that mean?"

The wise old cat slowly blinked open one eye to gaze at Ishmael. "Mouths speak many words," said Miat. "You must listen to many mouths to find the words you need to hear." The cool green eye blinked shut and old Miat was asleep again.

This didn't help Ishmael's muddle at all. He was still

confused. But he thought and he thought about what Miat had said. "Well I guess I'd better get busy listening to mouths," said Ishmael.

He wandered outside into the soft spring day. "Perhaps when I hear the right words, I will know who I am."

Ishmael wandered around and around the farmyard looking for mouths and listening for words. Pretty soon he spied the dogs lying in the warm soft dirt beside their doghouse.

Happily he trotted over to them, but they were not saying any words at all. They were fast asleep.

Ishmael wandered past the doghouse and into the barn. There were the big, black and white cows chewing, chewing, chewing on the hay. Ishmael thought to himself, "maybe their words will help."

He skipped eagerly over to them. The cows watched him kindly with soft brown eyes, but they did not say any words. They just kept on chewing the hay. Ishmael gave a big sigh, and said, "listening for words is very difficult."

Ishmael wandered out of the barn and down the hill behind it. The green grass felt good under his little feet. Ishmael frolicked along, running and skipping, kicking his spindly black legs in funny little jumps as lambs do. Every once in a while he would stop to nibble the grass. But, always, his soft pointy ears listened for mouths making words. When he reached the apple orchard he heard the bees busily buzzing among the pink blossoms.

"Buzz. . . buzz. . . buzz."— just one word, over and over, "buzz. . . buzz. . . buzz." Ishmael ran from tree to tree buzzing to the bees. But I'm afraid his buzzing sounded rather like "mazz. . . mazz." He made his mouth into a little circle and tried very hard to buzzzzzz. It still sounded like mazzzzzz. "Well, I must look for different mouths with different words," he said. So, he began to frolic again and to jump and to run.

As he ran down the hill toward the pond Ishmael heard many peeping sounds. "There are many words down there," he shouted. "I must hurry." He ran faster and faster down the hill. The peeping sounded loud in his ears. He was so excited he didn't even slow down when he reached the muddy edge of the pond. He was still listening to all those peeping words as he slid and fell and tumbled and even jumped

into the shallow pond. There Ishmael sat in the water, mud

splashed and quite wet, listening to the many, many mouths.

"It's so much fun to be a spring peeper," shouted Ishmael.

He opened his mouth wide, stuck out his little purple tongue,

and began to peep. "Peep. . . peep. . . peep," he sang. But,

Ishmael's peeping sounded very much like "maap. . . maap . . .

maap."

The dogs, still sleeping in the warm dirt beside their dog-house, awoke when they heard his excited cries. They thought he was calling for help, and they rushed down the hill.

What they found was a joyful little lamb sit-ting in the mud,

splashing water all about, and calling out, "maap. . . maap. . . maap." Ishmael was peeping as hard as he could!

"Why are you sitting in the mud little fellow, splashing

the water and crying out maap. . . maap. . . maap?" asked Bucky, the biggest of the dogs. "We were afraid you needed help."

"I'm practicing peeping with the other spring peepers," said Ishmael. "But it's very wet being a spring peeper."

The dogs ran back up the hill, laughing and shouting, "Ishmael thinks he's a spring peeper. What a silly fellow."

Ishmael sat in the mud a little while longer, splashing water and practicing peeping, but he was thinking about the laughing dogs. "I wonder why they think I'm silly. Perhaps I should ask them."

So, he got up out of the pond and shook himself a bit. He was still quite soggy as he trotted up the hill, through the apple orchard where the bees were still busily buzzing, to the yard where the dogs had curled up to continue their naps. Ishmael, tired from all that jumping into and out of the water, turned three times in a circle, and curled up too. He was full of questions, but as comfortable as a drowsy dog. He fell asleep.

When he awoke the dogs were chattering softly to each other. Ishmael lay there and lazily listened. As he did so he began to think about what old Miat had said. "Different mouths have different words. You

must listen with your heart to what your ears hear." He listened with his heart and he felt good. He was so content curled there in the dust with the other dogs that he said right out loud, "I'm so happy to be a dog!"

Bucky, the biggest dog, smiled at him and said, "If you are a dog, you must learn to take care of your family. You must bark when strangers come to the gate. You must let them know that you are guarding your farm."

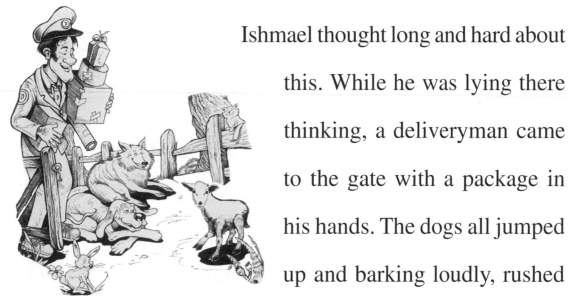

Ishmael thought long and hard about this. While he was lying there thinking, a deliveryman came to the gate with a package in his hands. The dogs all jumped up and barking loudly, rushed across the yard. Ishmael jumped up too. "I will help them guard the farm. I will show them what a good dog I am," he said as he ran with the dogs to the gate to bark at the stranger.

"Woof. . . woof," barked the dogs. "Maaf. . . maaf," barked Ishmael.

"Woof... woof... woof... maaf... maaf... maaf."

What a funny commotion they made. The dogs began to laugh. Even the deliveryman began to laugh. They all watched Ishmael as he barked and barked.

"Maaf. . . maaf. . . maaf. I like to be a dog. I like to guard my farm."

He stamped his foot to show them how much he meant it.

Two fluffy gray and white kittens, Huff and

Puff, were sitting on the fence nearby. They watched Ishmael stamping his foot and barking. It made them laugh too.

They ran along the fence and jumped off into the grass. Huff and Puff rolled and wrestled. As they tumbled about, they laughed little kitten sounds. They called out to Ishmael, "Why are you stamping your foot and saying maaf. . . maaf. . . maaf?"

"I'm barking," said Ishmael. "I'm guarding my farm with the other dogs."

The kittens laughed even more. They stopped their tumbling to say, "You don't sound very much like a dog. Come with us. You can be a kitten. You can help us chase a mouse."

So Ishmael ran to play with the kittens. They rolled and tumbled and wrestled, all the while sniffing here and sniffing there to find a mouse to chase.

"Oh, it's fun to be a kitten," thought Ishmael.

As they tumbled about playing in the yard, they rolled near the window where old Miat, the wisest one of all, watched from the window seat. Ishmael called up to him, "Mr. Miat, Sir, I've been searching very hard to find out who I am. I tried on Maa Maa's coat. I listened to many words. I helped the dogs guard the farmyard. I like being a dog, but everyone laughs when I bark. Do you think, perhaps, I might be a kitten? I like to play and tumble. I like to run."

Old Miat looked down from the window and said, "You must run down the right path to find your answer." And that is all he would say.

Ishmael was sitting under the window thinking about which path to follow when the kittens, Huff and Puff, came racing up to him calling, "Hurry, Ishmael. A mouse. A mouse. Help us chase the mouse."

Across the yard the three of them ran chasing the little mouse right through the flower patch, right through the washing hung so neatly on Mrs. Farmer's clothesline. Fast. . . faster down the path toward the barn they ran. Huff and Puff were laughing and calling, "Hurry, Ishmael, hurry."

Ishmael was running and jumping and shouting, "Oh, I love being a kitten. I love being a kitten."

Just in time, the little mouse spied a huge old oak tree by the barn door. He darted up into its leafy branches to hide from that whole noisy bunch. The kittens darted up right behind him. Ishmael skidded to a stop beneath the tree.

"I ran down the path with the other kittens," he thought. "I will

climb the tree too." He jumped onto the lowest branch.

"Watch out, little mouse, here I come," he shouted. He jumped from one branch onto another. And another. And then another. Up, up, high into the tree. As he was jumping so carefully from branch to branch, he saw Huff and Puff climb down the tree and hurry into the barn. Ishmael perched on a branch high in the treetop. He looked down, down, down. He sighed.

"Jumping up into the tree was quite easy, but I don't believe I can jump back down. Oh, my, whatever shall I do?"

As Ishmael stood on his branch high in the tip top of the old, oak tree, thinking about his problem, he heard a chittering, chirping sort of noise all about him. There was chirping in front of him and chirping behind him. There was some chirping above him and even below him. Tiny yellow birds, bright blue birds, brown and black and even orange birds flitted among the branches. They

zipped here and there playing hide and seek in the green leaves and golden sunshine, all the while chirping out their bird words.

"Hey little fellow, what are you doing sitting in the top of our tree?" they chirped to him.

"Well," Ishmael answered, "I was chasing a mouse. But the other kittens climbed down. I don't know how to get down. It is fun being a kitten, but it's not much fun just sitting here in the treetop. Whatever shall I do?"

"Come play with us," said the birds. "You'll like being a bird. We're having a wonderful game of hide and seek."

"I don't know how to be a bird," said Ishmael, "but, your game does look like fun."

"All you have to do," said the tiniest of the yellow birds,

"is aim for where you want to go, flap your wings and smoothly glide through the air. It feels so good . . . the air on your feathers! And then, just follow us. We'll show you how to dart in and out of the leaves. We'll have a wonderful game together. Come along, Ishmael. Play with us."

Ishmael watched the brightly colored birds for a few minutes. They were having such fun playing among the leaves. The sunshine was playing hide and seek too, sparkling through the leaves of the tree.

"I will. . . I will play hide and seek with the other birds in this beautiful tree," said Ishmael. He laughed right out loud. So, Ishmael aimed for where he wanted to fly. He flapped his spindly front legs, and he leaped happily right off his branch. Well, poor Ishmael didn't even have time to yell, "Oh, it's

fun to be a bird. I love being a bird." He just started falling right straight down. He flapped and he flapped, but his wings were spindly black legs, and instead of feathers, he had short brown hair. He couldn't swoop. He couldn't even glide. He could only fall straight down. And he did. . . down. . . down . . . down. . . right into the middle of a very large, very soft

haystack. My, what a surprise!

 The birds watched him from above. All around the haystack were many little animals just about his size.

They watched him, too, with their soft brown eyes. And all the time they were watching him, they were 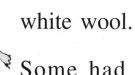 nibbling, nibbling, nibbling on the hay. Some of them had soft, curly coats of white wool. Some of the woolly coats were black. Some had white faces. Some had black faces. Some of them even had coats of short brown and black hair, just like Ishmael. They all had little pointy ears. They all had spindly legs and pointed feet. And they nibbled, and they nibbled and they nibbled, as all lambs do.

As Ishmael climbed out of the haystack they gathered

around him and asked, "What is your name, little lamb?"

Ishmael looked from one face to another. They smiled at him softly. All of a sudden Ishmael knew who he was.

"I am Ishmael Munch," he shouted. "I am a lamb. I'm a LAMB. I'm a perfectly fine little lamb. . . and my name is ISHMAEL MUNCH! I'm so happy to be a LAMB."

Then Ishmael and all the other lambs began to frolic around the haystack. Running and skipping. Kicking their legs in funny jumps and sometimes stopping to nibble the hay, as all lambs do.

Diane Ashley-Barlow was born and educated in Ann Arbor, Michigan. She served for 24 years as a Circuit Court Clerk in Washtenaw County, before retiring to a farm in Manchester, Michigan. She and her human family — son, Jesse, grandchildren, Bronwyn and Evan — are building a house on their farm which houses their animal family of 2 dogs, 7 cats, 2 donkeys, 3 llamas, 6 sheep and 9 goats.

Diane never intended to have this extended family of animals, but her reputation as a caregiver has caused people to bring animals to her — many sick or injured —for her to heal and love. And love is what keeps this wonderful lady and her animals together.

Diane has trained and shown dogs in breed rings, including Ottawa and Madison Square Garden. She enjoys training dogs to show and instructing others in obedience and tracking for search and rescue service.

Her "quiet" time includes spinning and weaving — many times using wool and fur from her own animals. She loves writing children's stories and poetry. Ishmael Munch, when little, accompanied her to classrooms. However, the most popular place to visit all of Diane's animals is on her farm in Manchester.